The Hill

OH what a day Series

C. Ardis

authorHOUSE®

AuthorHouse™
1663 Liberty Drive
Bloomington, IN 47403
www.authorhouse.com
Phone: 1-800-839-8640

Published by AuthorHouse 1/13/2012

ISBN: 978-1-4685-3699-7 (e)
ISBN: 978-1-4685-3700-0 (hc)
ISBN: 978-1-4685-3701-7 (sc)

Library of Congress Control Number: 2011963458

Any people depicted in stock imagery provided by Thinkstock are models, and such images are being used for illustrative purposes only. Certain stock imagery © Thinkstock.

This book is printed on acid-free paper.

Acknowledgments

Jesus, for my life
Mom, for your sacrifice
Tatiana and Shaeboy, my joy
April, thanks for believing
Jeffrey you are missed my friend.
Fourth man on The Hill
The best Dad I know.

Forward

Dear Fathers, Mothers, and lovely children. This is the first in a series of family adventures that my brother Chris, (a mover and shaker in the history of incredible kid adventures) is beginning to write down. There was a time, not long ago that we were young and we lived for different things than what grownups continually think about. Our jobs were to play and play hard and to invent things that no other kids had figured out before. On this first adventure, you are going to read about the big hill and a narrow escape from certain death, which became the subject of many other narrow escapes.

The night before the big hill incident, our mom made us our own little meatloaves covered in mashed potatoes and carved to look like igloos.

It was my second favorite meal memory. My first was having a big pile of homemade French fries for dinner. We dipped the salty fries in ketchup and thought it was the coolest meal ever. It was not until years later that our mother told us that a small bag of potatoes was all she had in the house to feed the six of us that day. However, we never went hungry and neither did anyone else who found our door. Mom would feed the Mexican people who showed up starving in our yard after a long journey across the border and kids knew they could always find something to eat at our table.

People would say that we were poor because of our lack of material things, but this never touched our hearts or broke the spirit of adventure that woke us up each morning. A distant relative asked me not long ago, how hard it must have been to live through the difficult times we had as kids. Our dad had abandoned us years before but our mother never did. She brought us to church on Sundays and taught us how to play baseball. We had an early model Oldsmobile that was often crammed with our family and every kid that showed up at our house in the morning on our way to the beach. And although we may have had intense tempers and tremendous battles with each other, no one else ever messed with the small fierce group that constituted the Ardis clan.

I am certain that our mother's guardian angels stopped up her ears so she was unaware of half the crazy things we were doing. I hope that these writings will be a pleasant surprise to her, but also will most likely be a shock. I think as she reads these tales, she may also smile a bit though.

As I picture our old neighborhood in Vista, California, I remember, climbing out at the bus stop and walking the ½ mile home, past fences loaded with climbing rose bushes, plumb and avocado fields, peaches that grew right below our property, tree houses that we built and slept in on warm summer nights and underground tunnels that we dug in the dirt pile next door. We would get off the bus, get a snack and be gone until mom called for us for dinner. "April, Michael, Christopher, Stephen, Kimberly time to eat."

There was many a day that blue-eyed Chris came home with his pockets full of lizards or rodents from the field behind our house and was sent back outside to reunite them with their families. My brothers put together bicycles from spare parts that broke world records on ramps built out of scrap wood in our driveway. Gladiator sports were played in the field behind our house while our old German shepherd refereed from the sidelines. Nights were spent in front of our three channel black and white TV watching The Wonderful World of Disney or The Courtship of Eddies Father, while the days revealed us as the Huck Fins and Tom Sawyers of the twentieth century.

At night mom was on the couch, the three boys were in one bedroom and my sister and I in another. The outside world may have told us we were deprived, but we did not have time to feel desperate - we were defying death on a daily basis and winning.

Every kid in the neighborhood wanted to be at our house. The boys would strategize the day's escapades with my younger sister Kim who was just as fearless as they were. I always followed behind watching to see what glory or disaster befell them. If they survived or for that matter were not taken to the hospital, I would try the newest trick. Soon the whole neighborhood would be talking about the crazy thing that happened at the small house down the street.

Today, we are all mothers, fathers and neighbors retelling stories at the dinner table during holidays that still bring tears to our eyes. I am grateful that Chris is writing down our family stories so that we can share them with other families. And our experience tells us that it is a relief to know in uncertain days, the sum of who we are does not consist of what we carry in our pockets or what the news may bring into our homes, or the labels that may be placed on us. Memories can still be made with those we love and retold or read to those who remember or want to remember what its like to be a child again.

April Gray (Number one sibling in the Ardis clan)

Shae, Chris, Tatiana

The Hill

It was just your typical Saturday morning in Vista, California, for most of the Ardis clan, save one. The sun was up and so was the gang—Mike, Chris, and, of course, Stanley Bailey (the wild kid at the end of the cul-de-sac). He was a wiry kid with long, straight, blond hair; thick, wire-frame glasses; and a twisted grin from ear to ear. Every daily event somehow became a challenge with either me or Mike.

Chris.

Well, the competitive juices were flowing that morning. Unknown to us, at the end of the cul-de-sac Stanley's day had already been planned out—long before the sun had set the previous evening. After we rolled out of bed and sat down at the breakfast table to polish off some cream of wheat, we stepped out onto our concrete porch, headed down the stairs to the carport area, and wondered what wonderful adventures awaited us.

We could risk it again and sprint across our driveway over to the dirt field to check out the place where, previously, a swarm of yellow jacket wasps had made a home in a long, corroded metal pipe. Maybe we could again jump up and down on the end and try to flush out the little yellow stinging bandits before they could corral us up and make dartboards out of us. I imagined it would be hard to fly through a rusty one-inch pipe while it was shaking, bust out of the opening, and try to deal with the pesky intruders, especially when the intruders would try to out run them.

I remember when my mom tried to warn us that messing with the yellow jackets would lead to getting stung. I just shrugged her off, though. "Ah, Mom, I'm too fast," was my quick and witty reply.

Yet she was proven right when my foot slid over the opening, causing me to land on the ground only to see the hive latch onto my face in a nanosecond. No, I had learned that painful lesson all too well. Check that one off.

Maybe we would take out our long, plastic, banana-colored belly scooter and bomb the vacant driveway on our neighbor's hill.

We could lie down flat on our stomachs and then proceed to shoot across the road with our eyes closed and (of course) without using the brakes, trying to avoid becoming roadkill between the passing cars below.

Mike.

Well, maybe not. Last time we tried that stunt Mike was almost served hot off the grill of some lady's Chevy Nova, which almost creamed the poor kid. The woman then abruptly proceeded to grab him by the ear, walk him up the hill, and yell at my mom to put the monkeys back in the cage. Ah, shoot! Mike just waited till she went down the road and did it again. Rebel.

We used to love to take our glass canning jars and flashlights and go explore the underground tunnels to hunt for these shiny black bugs that had this cool red underbelly. That fun ended after the old man up the street asked us what we had imprisoned in our glass jars.

"Oh, just some cool-looking black bugs," we said.

As he came over and surveyed our black arachnid captives a little more closely, his expression and our conversation quickly changed. He began looking at us with great curiosity and caution. "Boys, how did you catch them?" he asked.

"Oh, that was easy! We just shined the light on them and grabbed them by their backs. Then we threw 'em in the jars," I said nonchalantly with a proud smirk.

We once again found ourselves being grabbed by the arms and scolded all the way up the hill as we were marched to our poor mother. And that's when she discovered that Larry, Curly, and Moe had been capturing black widow spiders from their webs, because we thought they were just cool-looking bugs. Man, it's a good thing we had lids for those jars.

This Saturday morning's adventure, however, had already been formulated in the mind of Stanley. Before we wiped the sleep out of our eyes at seven o'clock and headed off down the road, he had already been up and waiting. As Mike and I were on our way down the steps, there he sat—that familiar lean silhouette perched on his seat, arms hanging over his bike handle bars with a steely eyed stare. The confident grin he wore on his face hinted at the dastardly deed he had formulated the night before.

We were curious why he hadn't just pulled up the driveway like he normally did. What, no quick head nod? No "hey"? Nope, this morning he wasn't going to set a tire on enemy soil. This challenge had to be agreed upon on neutral ground. With a look of conceit and a snicker in his grin, we figured something was up.

As we grabbed our bikes and slowly headed down the driveway toward Stanley, not a word was spoken. As we rolled up on our hogs, exchanging stares and trying to see who would draw down first, Stanley leaned over and in a quiet mocking voice simply said, "the hill."

A sudden shot of fear mixed with adrenaline slowly moved from our hearts through our veins, and as we ground our hands around our grips a little tighter and stared back at both friend and foe, we leaned over our bars and said, "You're on, man."

A quick bike check gave us a moment to consider a game plan against the current champ. This challenge could at least give one of us bragging rights for the next week and a tale to tell on our morning bus ride to Monte Vista Elementary School. Stanley, on the other hand, would be stewing in his bowl of defeat. But nothing came to mind for the moment. Yes, Stanley had the upper hand this morning, as he knew surprise was the ultimate key. Like a predator, he sensed a sudden ripple of panic that caught both Mike and I off guard.

Now remember—I said it was a typical day for the Ardis clan, save one. My youngest brother Steve always found himself in the shadows of his big brothers. He was the last picked for street ball and would sit along the sidelines watching Mike and I tear up the turf with stealth and light-footed moves that would have amazed Mercury Morris. That, however, would never again be a typical morning after this day.

Steve had rolled out of bed from his usual night of rocking back and forth on his bunk bed. You see, Steve couldn't get to sleep at night without rocking back and forth and lightly tapping his head on the cross plank that kept him safe from a sure plunge to the floor below.

Maybe it was his psychological way of testing the boundaries that kept him secure. Or maybe it was his frustration from always being picked last. Whatever the case, after today, there would be no need for a safety bar on his bunk ever again.

Steve hopped out of bed and headed down to the kitchen to devour his favorite cereal—Cap'n Crunch with Crunch Berries. He would soon discover, however, that his golden bowl of happiness would be void of those delicious round red berry delights, because Mike and I had already picked the box clean of the Crunch Berries.

"That's it, man!" Steve replied, as he had finally reached his breaking point.

Yes, it was another poke; another perfectly delivered double jab from Mike and me that would soon play itself out in a most dramatic fashion. Steven noticed there was no rustle or noise that morning from the other room, but a quick bed check would be all the ammo Steve needed. This morning he was hunting for bear.

After finishing his Cap'n Crunch (with no Crunch Berries), Steve must have walked out to our carport, and not seeing the two other bikes next to his, the search was on.

He picked up his trusty blue bike (the same one that would bring him to his crowning moment) and headed down the long driveway. He made his usual right-hand turn to Stanley's house where we had built a dirt BMX track in the open field. Yet all along I knew there was something spinning in the back of Steve's mind as he was peddling alone (Lee Crewer), but we will get back to that shortly.

Dropping down the hill to our main street, Avocado Drive, Steve had to make a clear decision. Take a right, head down to the trails, and continue to the famed turnaround that ended Avocado Drive, or take a left and have two dilemmas that could institute a sudden panic and an unwanted predicament.

Hold on a minute. I told you we would get to Lee Crewer shortly. So Steve chose the obvious right. It was as Steve headed down past the trails and for the turnaround where the big knotted pepper tree stood as a stark landmark of remembrance that a certain hair-raising flashback must have crept in, no doubt. Let me explain.

A month or so earlier I had landed my first job as a professional news distributor (okay, fine—paperboy) of about thirty papers with the *Vista Press*. Well, I felt like Huck Finn having to spend his Saturday painting the long white picket fence and getting rather bored. In the story, Huck had come up with a plan to con some of his friends into grabbing a paintbrush and sharing in the same privilege he was enjoying, all while he sat back with a rather satisfying smirk and basked in his cleverness. Well, you remember the story I think!

Being cut from the same cloth of opportunity and cunning wit, the grey matter began to flow, and as the gears were greased and spinning, a dastardly plan came to my mind, which would soon play itself out on a beautiful Vista summer day.

Let me take you back for a brief moment and lay this slippery set up out for you. On my first week of being a paperboy for the *Vista Press*, I was down to my last paper. What a relief, or so I thought. As I peddled up the very last, long driveway and proceeded to hang a perfect shot on the front porch, all of my greatest fears came to the forefront.

You see, when you're a paperboy, two of the greatest fears are meeting the neighborhood bully and meeting the hounds from—well, you know where. As my perfect strike hit its target and the sound reverberated through the screen, instant panic and the thought of death became eminent.

Busting through the door in unison as fast as greased lightning and not caring what the front page read, they hit the screen door like three linemen hitting a tackling dummy. I must have looked like a sixty-pound milk bone in the path of some midday canine cuisine. (Bone Appetite.)

Time stood still for a fraction of a second, and what my mind played before me will forever be etched in the halls of "lesson learned."

Fear has a way of getting you going, and panic has a way of setting you up for the worst. As I came out of my coma of chaos vision, I swung my bike around faster than Chuck Connors could reel off rounds from his rifle and tried to pedal faster than any human has pedaled in history. All seemed to be going well in that split moment. And then I felt the first clamp, then the second to my paperboy sash, all setting me up for the grand buttocks bite by the big, black Doberman of death. (Well planned, boys. Well planned.) In an instant, my stamina kicked in, and the teeth-mongering mutants that were now being dragged behind me let go of their near-death grips.

Shortly after that hair-raising experience, after barely surviving the jaws of defeat (while feeling victorious), a new sense of adventure had begun. I was selfishly convinced this was much too good to experience alone. Each day of my beastly encounter I began to use my subtle tactics that the hounds just couldn't seem to counter. Stealth was the key—that, and a nasty, curling, old English toss that raked the wind like a perfect boomerang at about thirty feet. Heck, by the time the newspaper hit its designated mark and the sound had made its way into the hound's arena, I was already down the road whistling a new tune of victory.

I was soon infused with sheer excitement to share my newfound exercise of death ritual on an unsuspecting fellow human being. But who? And more importantly, how? Well, yes, oh yes. The light had just come on, and Steve had just come in. In life every kid has some kind of weakness. Being his brother, and through years of careful observation, I knew how to bait the buttery trap that Steve just couldn't resist.

You see, about every other month my mom would give one of us boys a buck to head down to the local Wonder Bread Store and pick up a box of a dozen Hostess Twinkies. Yes, you heard me—a whole dozen.

So whoever she chose would get to have an extra one to bring in his lunch. That soft moist cake with that sweet creamy white filling would just be too tempting for Steve to turn down. So now the cheese was set in the trap and ready to be sprung.

It was my turn to ride down and get the creamy sponged delights and then return home to the waiting mouths of the hungry nesters. And that's when my plan suddenly—and skillfully, I might add—began to unfold. As I carefully picked the magic moment when the rest of the clan was preoccupied, I spoke up.

"Hey, Steve, see this extra Twinkie?" I began. "It's yours if you help me tomorrow on my route."

Hypnotized by the prospect of yet another heavenly, cream-filled moment, his eyes got as big as saucers. "Okay," he agreed. *The poor kid had no clue what he was about to face at 4:45 this time tomorrow.*

So the next day, as my evil plan began to unfold, we carelessly delivered each paper. As we were getting down to the last couple of customers, there must have been two diametrically opposed frames of mind. For Steve, the joy and delight of a creamy moist Twinkie on two consecutive days was just too good to believe. For me, knowing Steve would actually look like an oversized, vanilla cream-filled Twinkie to the hounds from—well, you know— would be, well, just as satisfying.

As the anticipation grew (for me) and we were down to our last two customers, I told Steve I had to take a left and go way up the hill. I offered him the last paper and told him to take it down the dirt driveway. I added that he needed to be sure to throw it on the porch, because they were really old and couldn't walk down the driveway to pick it up.

With that, the poor kid pedaled off, thinking to himself, *Oh man, one more paper, and then I get my golden treat at the end of the rainbow!*

Okay, okay, I know what some of you are thinking. *Dude, that was cold.* But others, those of you with little brothers, are thinking, *Brilliant.* Hurry now, and let's get back to the carnage.

So in reality, my customer was actually the second house on the left, and as soon as I dropped the paper on the driveway, I hustled back to the turnaround point by the end of the fence line to wait for that little sound that would get the wheels of sheer terror rolling. And then I heard it hit. But what I heard and what Steve saw coming at him could never be communicated. No, I was convinced it had to be experienced to be fully appreciated.

After failing to make a meal out of me and frustrated that I had eluded their plan of daily destruction, the hounds were perched and huddled tightly behind the screen door, focused and ready for their new, unsuspecting victim. The second the paper hit the porch, they were off. White sparkling teeth were set for fine dining, slobber filled every hole in the road, and yes, the horrible scream that shattered windows in two counties was now at full volume.

The careful planning and anticipation of my treacherous plan was now unfolding beautifully right before my eyes.

But then came the surprise of all surprises. I don't
know how Steve did it, but he flew right past me,
leaving a thin dust cloud that followed the driveway
all the way back to the house.

What?! The little runt had made it through the hounds' gauntlet without a stinking scratch, a chewed up extremity, or even a tear in his pant leg. How unfulfilling was my return on such an epically devious plan that was sure to be satisfied with the carnivorous carnage of the youngest pup of the family. Well, the only thing that got chewed on that night was my backside when Mom returned home and found out what had happened. Yes, my devious plan had ultimately backfired, and I was the one whose backside got eaten up—only to look up and see Steve smiling as he reaped the fruit of his heavenly, cream-filled reward.

So now, for Steve, this monumental journey would head back the opposite way to—yes, you know what's coming—dilemma number one: Lee Crewer. Lee was the neighborhood bully who lived to make kids' lives a constant horror story. He had curly red hair, peppered dry skin, a couple of chipped teeth, and a mouth like a garbage disposal. That didn't mix well with Steve's inability to keep his trap shut, and it was only a matter of time before the two were destined to hit head on.

About a week before Steve's crowning moment on the hill, as we were riding home from school, the bus unloaded kids about two or three stops from our stop. Guess who was on the street ready to terrorize kids for their extra lunch change or anything left over from their lunch boxes? Yep, you guessed it.

Well, Steve was feeling quite safe in his orange, oversized, armored chariot. He shot to the other side of the bus, and before we could stop him, he shouted as loud as he could, "Woman face," and laughed. Come to think of it, Steve was the only one laughing as the rest of the bus's occupants were huddled in the seats to avoid being seen or counted as an accomplice and risk suffering the painful consequences that were soon to be dished out.

Steve thought it was quite funny until he read the concern on the rest of our faces. As we raised our fingers in unison to point out back of the bus's window, Steve instantly knew he was a goner.

Lee was so mad that he looked like a locomotive steamer following the bus as fast as he could. Steve's face and those two words fueled the fire, and there was no running out of steam for Lee, yet the tracks for Steve were soon to end.

With only two stop signs to go before our stop, Steve knew Lee wouldn't be far behind. He moved to the front of the bus to try to get a head start that could quite possibly preserve his very life. We yelled over at the poor midday sacrifice and said, "Man, you'd better run as fast as you can 'cause we ain't helping you. He's too big and crazy to boot!"

Steve knew this would have to be the dash of his life, and as the bus slowed down, Steve was crouched at the front ready to exit like the poor guy in Lynyrd Skynyrd's "Gimme Three Steps" hit single. As the bus stopped and Gus the bus driver opened up the glass door for our exit, Steve hurdled the bus's three black steps and shot out like a greyhound with Woman Face in hot pursuit.

"Poor kid," Mike and I both said as Lee passed the bus's left-hand side. All we saw was the back of a skinny kid with a blonde bobble head and ankles screaming for momma.

Well, the inevitable happened. Woman Face caught up to him on Mr. Jack's driveway and punched him in the stomach. "What, no smart remark? No clever comment? Huh, smart aleck," Lee yelled.

Steve didn't say a word. Well, at least not till he got over the fence. Then, low and behold, guess what happened. At the top of his lungs, Steve screamed out once again, "Woman face!" We had to hand it to him. The kid had guts, although they were a little soar at the moment.

Knowing all of that, Steve journeyed down the road cautiously, body tense, ready to shift from low to turbo in a fraction of second. His eyes were peeled like a cat, with every strange sound inviting some horrific scenario. But, hey, so far so good. There was no crazy, curly-headed Crewer looking for a day to fill his Saturday slot with a certain sick torment of the youngest Ardis brother. No bushes rustling with a waiting ambush by the crazed madman.

The coast was clear, and the stage was now set for that which lurked around the next corner.

Dilemma number two would be even worse if Steve chose it. The hill on Hanaliea Drive was the testing ground for any kid to bomb, and as intimidating as Stanley Bailey was, the view to the bottom caused most kids to turn around or pass out on the spot.

As Steve rounded the corner, huffing and puffing up the hill, little did Mike, Stanley, and I know Steve was soon to become the man of the hour. With his tight cotton T-shirt and pants that came up six inches above his PRO-Keds, he ate up the distance like a tortoise.

We had been watching traffic with a keen eye, testing the wind, drawing our visual lines, drumming up every ounce of courage, making sure every muscle was willing and ready.

I was on the inside lane, Mike was in the middle, and Stanley was on the outside lane (his favorite), He owned the hill, so he got first choice. If you wimped out early, you could pull into the Methodist church on the left and wait for another day.

As we fixed our gaze to down below and evened out our front tires together, just inches apart, there was suddenly a fourth rider on the line.

With his eyes now fixed straight ahead and wide open, he dared not look over into the lions' den.

We only gave him a quick glance and no respect, because we thought he'd just come to watch, but in Steve's mind, he had conquered the hounds, survived a smackdown from Woman Face, and was now ready for what could possibly be the crescendo in his cap, the ultimate trifecta, the Hanaliea hat trick—if he could pull it off. Yes, the day of his personal reckoning before the older braves had arrived. Yet, what Steve was about to unknowingly face, few men would have contemplated.

The Challenge

So here was the challenge. We would all start in a line at the same time, and it only seemed like moments before we hit what felt like one hundred miles per hour. As your eyes began to water something fierce and you felt every bump and twitch in the road, you had to be fully prepared for cars pulling out of the Buena Vista Little League Field. After all, there was no way to stop in time if they did. And all this time you realized that at the bottom of the hill there was an impossible hairpin turn of certain death that no kid was prepared to take on. So, whoever summoned up enough courage and hit his brakes last was determined king of the hill for a week or so. You could always see the long skid marks from the previous challenge drawing closer, which meant you could push the envelope a little farther each time if you so felt the courage to do so.

The Final Leg

And then, without a sound, a dropped flag, or a starting gun, we began the impossible in full, tucked position. I got the early jump and was out front by about two bike lengths; Stanley was a

close second with Mike closing in fast. As we approached the halfway point, I felt a sudden game-changing shake from my front forks (go figure). Devastated by this new dilemma, I had to pull off to the church parking lot and commit to third place (or so I thought).

Mike and Stanley were neck and neck, and it came down to who was going to brake first. As they flew past the church, heads tucked down over their crossbars, tires humming in harmony and growing louder, suddenly, to my surprise—no, to my amazement—something quickly distracted my focus from the pack's final moments. I found myself frozen in silent wonder. Maybe it was just disbelief at what—or, better yet, who—I watched speed into the competition! Steve somehow found the courage, the grit, and the foolishness to take on the alpha males of the pride that morning.

As I studied the situation, something seemed to be terribly wrong. As Steve passed the halfway point, it was not only what I saw but what I heard that caught my attention. Why was he peddling backward? And then it hit me. Before I could believe my eyes, my ears heard the horrifying sound of Steve's chain dragging, scraping the ground below him.

You see, our bikes only had back brakes. There were no front brakes, so I guess Steve thought that if he could peddle backward, maybe he could reattach the chain. All the while, as he was trying to peddle, he was moaning over and over, "Oh no, no, no. Oh no, oh no."

His eyes were no doubt locked on the hairpin corner below, which was coming closer and closer. Just maybe he thought he could rewind this horrible nightmare that he couldn't wake up from. Of course, it was a hopeless endeavor as Steve was wide awake and headed for certain demise. Just ahead, Mike and Stanley simultaneously locked their brakes to a symphony of screeching, screaming, and smoking rubber tires.

As the smoke cleared and Mike and Stanley leaned over the front of their bars, their tires were exactly even.

For the first time ever, it was a dead heat. But before they could relish in their sudden historical moment, true history was about to be shattered.

Suddenly, something passed between them; for a moment it seemed unthinkable. It just couldn't be. Yes, it was. The horror of it all was only momentary as they also heard and observed what was quickly going to get ugly for Steve.

I was hauntingly perched with a bird's-eye view of the whole scenario that was quickly going to get ugly for Steve, yet, I couldn't get a single word out.

Point of No Return

Passing the skid marks that were held in the halls of quiet reverence by the Avocado Street Gang, and especially by Stanley Bailey, who held what seemed to be an unchallengeable mark. Everyone thought that Stanley's record would live through infamy, but it was about to not only be challenged on this day but demolished by the kid with the drooling disposition. There was no turning into the church (too far past it), there was no heading into the ditch on either side of the road, and there was no possible way he was going to make the turn at such speed.

You see, total and complete panic had now set in. Every useable body part was now locked—no, petrified—in an immovable position. Today a crown was to be given out, a seat of respect, a tale that every kid from a fifty-mile radius would chime out. Steve was about to become *"the* kid." Fathers would sit around the campfire, or dinner table, and pass this epic story on to their sons and spill out every stomach-curling detail as if they were at ground zero.

Yes, Steve had somehow pulled a Harry Houdini and miraculously survived the canine fly trap—unscathed and without a single scratch. He had also lived through the bashing of the neighborhood bully's wrath. This time, however, Steve had bitten off more than he could chew. In a few more seconds he would taste the bitter pill and pay the ultimate price for his moment of fame. Yes, in a few bleak seconds, waiting to welcome him would be more pain than he could have ever imagined or thought was possible to endure.

Was it worth all the glory to make a name among the pack or to relish and bask in the applause and approval from every other kid who had stood atop that mount only to chicken out and cower back home in shameful defeat? Well, soon enough we were going to find out, knowing that no matter how hard Steve pedaled that chain, it wasn't going to jump back on the sprocket. The only thing that wasn't going to move today on impact was the quickly approaching, squirrel-infested dirt bank that was willing and ready to swallow the poor kid alive.

Scream Scene

Then came the scream that seemed to deafen every natural and unnatural sound within a mile of its epicenter. As men, women, and children headed for cover, as windows broke and cats shimmied up any available tree, as the blue blaze of misery forged ahead like Jethro Tull's "Locomotive Breath," as Johnny pulled the handle and the train it can't stop rolling no it couldn't slow down. The cheering crowd at Buena Vista ballpark was suddenly distracted from watching Ferman Cardoza hit his league-leading twentieth home run on the lower field. The kids waiting to catch the ball on the railroad tracks above froze in disbelief at the blazing blue bike rider breaking the sound barrier and the cry of terror at what was about to unfold. The grim reaper's knees were even heard to have buckled from the shrieking howl.

As the blue blaze of misery screamed ahead, the deafening pitch began peeling back paint from every home's exterior and leaving every green leaf withering in its wake. At Steve's building, thunderous speed, there was no way of making (or surviving) Hanaliea's hairpin corner. Steve knew it would either be certain death or the worst case of road rash in his life, which left only one choice.

He would have to slowly steer (or lean) slightly left, then straighten out, and set a course directly into the squirrel-infested bank that must have had at least a thousand holes.

As the pitch of the scream of all screams reached its zenith, suddenly it became clear—the colony of our furry little friends had now caught wind of the young man's dilemma. Squirrels that had once been enjoying their Saturday morning playing in the sun, scurrying about to catch a morsel from the ballfield's trash cans, or hiding underneath the bleachers were suddenly alerted to the sound of a possible cataclysmic destruction ahead.

In one accord, the peaceful colony of furry-tailed locals built holes into the hillside began digging, scratching, and burrowing at a feverish pitch, foreseeing a human projectile's unintended path of carnage heading straight for them. It was clear—dig or face the alternative. The ultimate party crasher was on his way in without an invitation or a bucket of KFC to share.

The Launch

And then it happened—a little dip in the road, a small ripple in the asphalt, was all it took to turn the wheel a hard left. He was off, in flight over the curb and straight into the bank, headfirst.

Yes, a direct hit into the bank's belly.

The impact was so great it sent pressure through every squirrel families' dwelling. As the pressure quickly moved through each tunnel, it rained furry little critters for about five seconds due to the impact.

To this day, the mystery of a measured ground movement on the seismograph still boggles the professors at Berkeley and remains a mystery.

A plume of fine, soft dirt rose like a mushroom cloud as kids ran to the edge of the outfield fence and waited as the dust settled to see if there were any signs of life or movement. Then, suddenly, like a champagne bottle being uncorked, out came the body and head not of a boy, but of a man. Steve had miraculously accomplished the impossible and would always and forever stand alone as the one and only King of the Hill.

The Crowning

As Steve gazed up the hill, his mind desperately tried to rewind the events that had just taken place and he checked every body part, which he found to miraculously be still in place. He spotted the petrified group of spectators halfway up the hill, who were clearly still in disbelief at this unbelievable spectacle; words were just not appropriate. Only in one's imagination could a feat such as this even be concocted, let alone survived.

Realizing he was still alive and breathing, his tear-stained face caked with the native soil, his hair barely visible through the finely compacted dust, and his eyes wide open, Steve actually looked like one of the little critters.

Yes, the trifecta was now checked off and complete, and for all time was never to be repeated.

We met Steve at the bottom of the hill, but we were stunned into absolute silence. Not a word was spoken that day as Steve (for the first time) led the pack home. We didn't mind walking and coasting all the way home, because what we had just witnessed would play over and over in our memory banks for years to come. Kids around the block were amazed as they heard what had never been thought possible, and Steve had now set his mark and received his title of King of the Hill.

What we had just seen even erased our heroes' highlights from the past. Fonzie jumping over the shark tank (rubbish), Evil Knievel at Caesar's Palace (yawn), Wide World Sports Agony of Defect (boring)—they were all minimized to a nursery rhyme compared to the history made at Hanaliea hill by the unlikeliest of all. Yes, and every day thereafter was a fourth man on the hill, and he was welcome.

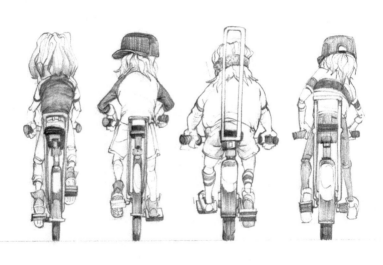

Excerpt from "The Beast"

There was no way of stopping or avoiding a most painful and gruesome outcome, as we entered the ditch of death at about 35 or 40 miles per hour. Pour Linda didn't even see what was coming, but she would soon painfully learn you don't need wings to be able to fly.

About the Author

These stories are about my life and my families lives growing up in a single parent home in the 60"s and 70's and the daily adventures we found ourselves in (or created) and the characters who played out the scenes that you will soon read about,so get ready for some fun and lots of riveting action,and laughter..as the Avocado street gang whips you up in an modern day Huckleberry Finn classic..

I want to be able to communicate that even a family of five 3 boys and 2 girls living at the poverty level with my Mom, regardless of Her circumstances reinforced Love,sacrifice,discipline,and lots of wonderful fun memories as we would pack up the old rambler with a half tank of gas and 10 bucks in her pocket and enjoy life as a family together no matter where we went..

I still live in wonderful sunny San Diego california only 20 minutes from my old neighborhood in Vista california.I still talk with my old friends growing up,mom is now Living in Julian,home of the famous apple pies,all of us are still here and close and I have spent the last 20 years in youth ministry and coaching at my local church and high school.I want to be able always to give back and have a huge heart for the single moms and dads out there that are really being amazing parents though they live paycheck to paycheck,in a small apartment,limited on things they can involve their kids in,but showing them how to be a great model in the community,a servant in there community,and a person of character..I still have that wild streak in me and ride motocross,surf,sn owboard,skate,pretty much everything with a ball. Love more than anything helping others succeed in life and sharing my Christian faith to all by serving..